Jessica Souhami studied at the Central School of Art and Design. ... 1980 she formed
Mme Souhami & Co, a travelling puppet company using colourful shadow puppets with
a musical accompaniment ... storyteller. Her first book for Frances Lincoln was
The Leopard's Drum, fol... *Sunday*
Telegraph said of her tw... ...aught
a Flea, "Graphically bol... and fun".
Her most recent titles ... story
written by Alison Lurie ... *the*
Dark, Dark Wood and *N...* ... in
collaboration with the ...

The Famous Adventure of
A Bird-Brained Hen

Jessica Souhami

FRANCES LINCOLN

I'm going to tell you the famous story
of a bird-brained hen called Penny.

And this is how it goes…

One day an acorn fell, BOP!
on Henny Penny's head.

"OOF," she said. "What was that?"
And she looked up.
"The sky must be falling," she said.
"I must go and tell the King."
So Henny Penny hurried along.
And very soon…

...she met Ducky Daddles.
"Hello," said Daddles.
"Where are you going?"

"I'm going to tell the King
that the sky is falling," said Penny.

"You can come too."

So Henny Penny and
Ducky Daddles hurried along.

And very soon…

…they met Cocky Locky.
"Hello," said Locky. "Where are
you two going?"

"We're going to tell the King that the sky is falling," said Penny and Daddles. "You can come too."

So Henny Penny, Ducky Daddles
and Cocky Locky hurried along.
And very soon…

…they met Goosey Poosey.
"Hello," said Poosey.
"Where are you three going?"

"We're going to tell the King that the sky is falling," said Penny and Daddles and Locky. "You can come too."

So Henny Penny, Ducky Daddles,
Cocky Locky and Goosey Poosey
hurried along.

And very soon…

…they came to Foxy Loxy's house.

And there was Foxy Loxy at the door.

"Hello!" said Foxy.

"Where are you all going?"

"We're going to tell the King that the sky is falling," said Penny and Daddles and Locky and Poosey. "But *somehow* we've come to your door."

"Quite right!" said Foxy.
"This *is* the quickest way to the
King's Palace. DO COME IN!"
And they were just about to enter
Foxy's house…when….

...Henny Penny peeped inside.
And she saw –

a cooking pot full of boiling water,
a carrot and an onion, neatly chopped,
AND, glinting behind Foxy's back...
the sharp, sharp edge of a big, big
CHOPPER!

"OH NO!" she cried.
"We're for Foxy's SOUP!"
"QUICK BIRDS, FLY!"

And they did!

And back at home, ruffled but safe,
Henny Penny decided not to go to the
King to tell him that the sky was falling.
Well, not today.

And as for Foxy Loxy…
all he had for dinner
was some
very thin
soup.

And that is the end of the story.

First published in Great Britain in 2003 by

Frances Lincoln Limited, 4 Torriano Mews

Torriano Avenue, London NW5 2RZ

w.w.w.franceslincoln.com

First paperback edition 2004

British Library Cataloguing in Publication Data available on request

ISBN 0-7112-2025-5 hardback

ISBN 0-7112-2026-3 paperback

Set in Gill Sans

Printed in Singapore

9 8 7 6 5 4 3 2 1

OTHER PICTURE BOOKS FROM FRANCES LINCOLN

OLD MACDONALD

Jessica Souhami

Old MacDonald's farm is full of surprises. What's that in the pram?
Who's flying a plane? Lift the flaps and see for yourself.
Selected for Child Education Best Books of 1996

Suitable for National Curriculum English – Reading, Key Stage 1
Scottish Guidelines English Language – Reading, Talking and Listening, Level A
ISBN 0-7112-1086-1

SILLY RHYMES SERIES:
MOTHER CAUGHT A FLEA
ONE POTATO, TWO POTATO

Jessica Souhami

Two books of much-loved playground rhymes and chants: Two fat sausages,
Burger in a bun, I'm the king of the castle and many more all-time favourites.

Suitable for Nursery Level, and for National Curriculum English – Reading and Listening, Key Stage 1
Scottish Guidelines English Language – Talking and Listening, Level A
ISBN Mother Caught a Flea 0-7112-1243-0
ISBN One Potato, Two Potato 0-7112-1244-0

IN THE DARK, DARK WOOD

Jessica Souhami

There's something really spooky in the dark, dark wood. Where is it hiding?
What can it be? Turn the pages and lift the flaps to search the house. As you go,
cheeky creatures play hide-and-seek with you, but a scary hand still beckons…

Suitable for Nursery and Early Years Education
Scottish Guidelines English Language, Level A
ISBN 0-7112-1540-5

Frances Lincoln titles are available from all good bookshops
Or visit our website www.franceslincoln.com